Check out these other exciting STECK-VAUGHN Science Fiction Titles!

How far would you go to break into
the movies? Get the answer in
BEHIND THE SCREAMS

Here today . . . gone tomorrow!
Find out more in
WARP WORLD 3030

Earth is in for a big jolt. Check out why in
SHORT CIRCUIT

There's a whole lot of shakin' going on!
Read all about it in
SUPER STAR

What *are* those robots talking about?
Find out in
THE LOST LANGUAGE

All that glitters isn't good! See why in
CHARMERS

History can really get to you! Learn more in
BLAST FROM THE PAST

You may get more than you bargained for!
Check out
COSMIC EXCHANGE

This fan is out of this world!
Find out why in
ALIEN OBSESSION

ISBN 0-8114-9322-9

2 3 4 5 6 7 8 9 98 97 96

Produced by Mega-Books of New York, Inc.
Design and Art Direction by Michaelis/Carpelis Design Assoc.

Cover illustration: Matthew Archambault

BZZZZ

by Ann Weil

interior illustrations by
Marie DeJohn

STECK-VAUGHN
COMPANY

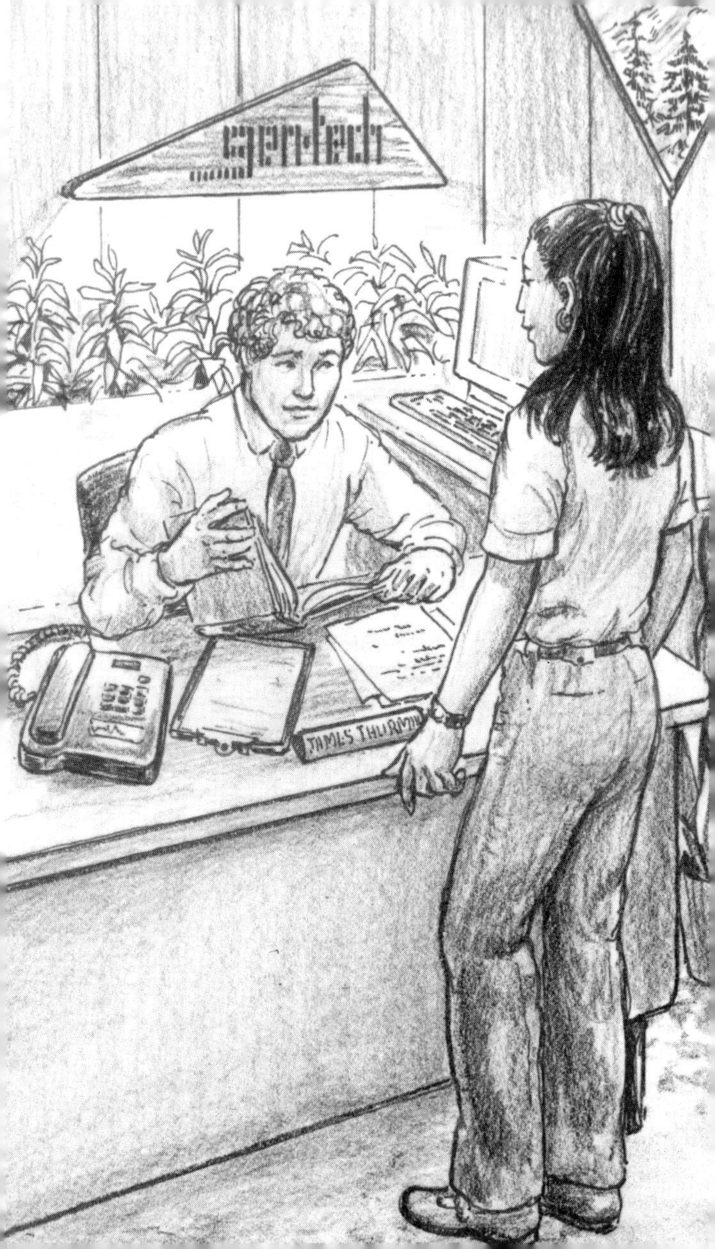
gentech

Chapter · 1

Tanya Redfeather walked into Gen-Tech Laboratories with her head held high and her back as straight as an arrow. She could feel her heart racing.

"Remember, Tanya," her grandmother had said over breakfast. "If you act confident, you will be confident."

Tanya knew it was good advice. But like most advice, it was a lot easier said than done.

She walked toward the receptionist, a friendly-looking young man with sandy brown hair. Tanya noticed he was reading a college science textbook.

He glanced up as she approached.

"May I help you?" the young man asked.

"I'm Dr. Troy's new intern," Tanya replied.

"Oh, yes." The receptionist looked through a few papers on his desk. "Tanya Redfeather," he said with a friendly smile. "What an interesting name you have."

Tanya smiled back. She glanced at the nameplate on his desk: James Thurman.

"Here," James said. He handed Tanya a clipboard with several forms attached to it. "You need to complete these forms. Then, you may go downstairs to get your ID badge."

"Thanks," Tanya said. She took the clipboard and sat down in one of the boxy chairs in the reception area. She started to fill out the forms, writing in the date, June 1, 2001.

Most of the questions required little thought. Tanya filled in her name, age, place of birth, and so on.

EMPLOYMENT FORM

JUNE 1, 2001

Name: _____

Age: _____

Place of birth: _____

Parent or
guardian: _____

But Tanya paused for a moment before filling in the line that asked for her "parent or guardian." Tanya's parents had died when she was just a baby. Her grandmother had taken care of her ever since then. Tanya wrote in her grandmother's name on the line. Then she checked over the form.

When Tanya was finished, she handed the clipboard and papers back to James.

He was on the phone, but he briefly looked up at Tanya as he took the clipboard.

"Yes," James said into the phone, "she's here now." He listened for a moment. "Okay. I will. Thanks. Bye."

James hung up the phone and flipped through the forms. "These look fine to me. You can go downstairs now. The security officer is expecting you," he added.

James pointed towards the end of the corridor. "That elevator will take you to Subbasement 3. When you get out of the elevator, take the first left, then make another left. The security office will be on your right."

"Thanks," Tanya said. She headed for the elevator, repeating James's instructions to herself.

"See you later," James called as Tanya stepped into the elevator. The doors closed behind her.

Even though she was nervous, Tanya was excited about her summer internship at Gen-Tech. It was one of the best research centers in all of Canada.

Gen-Tech was only a few miles from the small town where Tanya lived with her grandmother. Tanya's grandmother was a full-blooded Ingalik. She was the medicine woman for her tribal community and for several other Athabascan tribes in that part of western Canada.

Tanya's grandmother wanted Tanya to learn the traditional ways of her ancestors. Tanya really valued her grandmother's teachings, but she was also interested in studying modern science, especially biology.

Tanya had recently been reading about current developments in genetic research. Tanya could imagine herself working in a laboratory like Gen-Tech. She saw herself in the lab, working to create new crops that would need less water. Or she could cross-breed new vegetables to create new high-energy foods.

Tanya knew biology and technology could work together to help improve life for a lot of people. That's why she had applied for this summer internship back in September, at the beginning of her

junior year in high school.

Over three hundred high school juniors from all over Canada had applied. Tanya was surprised when she was called for a personal interview with Dr. Katherine Troy herself.

Dr. Troy had been very businesslike. She had asked Tanya many questions about her school work and home life.

Usually Tanya didn't talk about her grandmother's work with traditional medicine. It wasn't that Tanya was embarrassed by her grandmother. In fact, she was very proud of her. It was just that many people didn't believe in traditional healing. Some people even made fun of Tanya's grandmother, calling her a witch doctor.

But during the interview, Dr. Troy seemed sincerely interested in Tanya's grandmother's work as an herbalist. Tanya was impressed by how much Dr. Troy knew about herbs and other natural medicines.

Dr. Troy had explained that spending so much time in the rain forests studying insects had taught her a respect for nature. Sometimes, she had to rely on medicinal plants to relieve minor problems, since there were no doctors or drugstores within hundreds of miles. Dr. Troy had also told Tanya about all the medicines that were products of the rain forest.

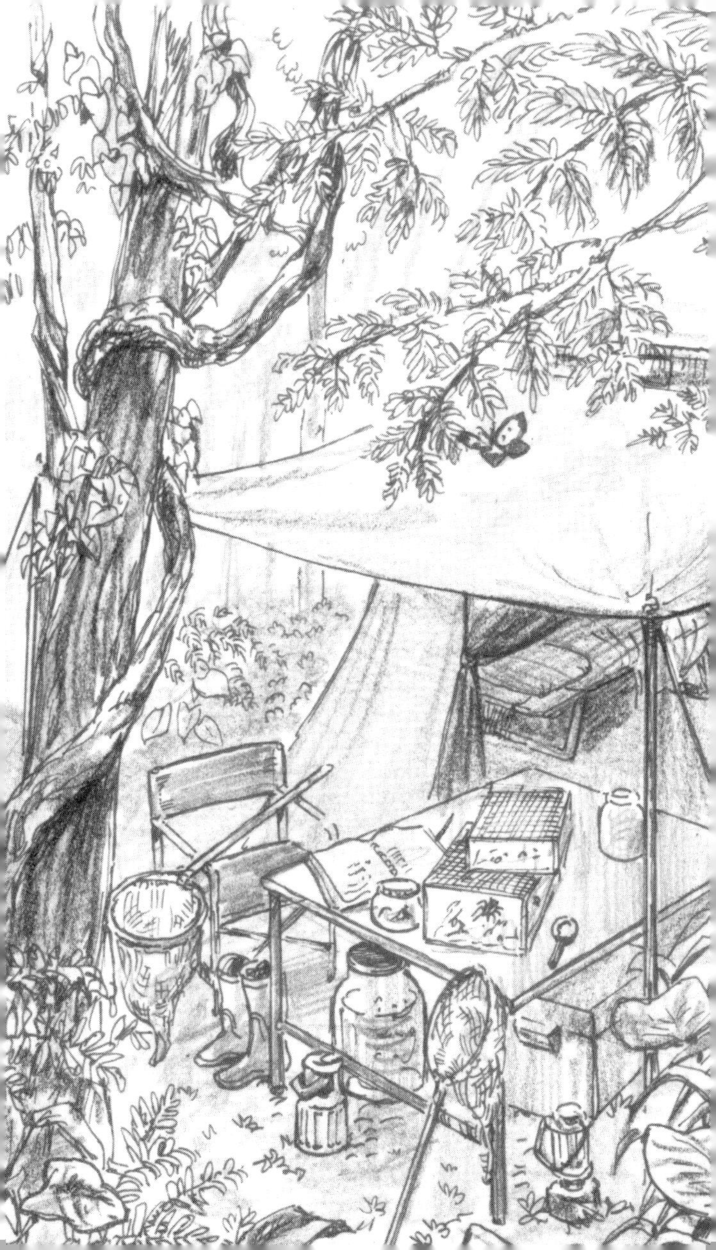

The elevator opened and Tanya found her way to the security office. The security officer, Ms. Fletcher, was a plump woman with a no-nonsense attitude. Soon Tanya was wearing an ID badge around her neck.

Ms. Fletcher explained how to use the ID badge.

"Put the badge up against the metal door plate," Ms. Fletcher explained. "That will release the lock. Then you can push the door open."

Tanya's badge gave her access to Dr.

Troy's lab and to most of Gen-Tech's common areas: the cafeteria, the lounge, and the rest rooms. But there were many places that were off-limits. Tanya's badge would not open doors to those high-security areas.

"You're all set now," said Ms. Fletcher. She shook Tanya's hand. "Welcome to Gen-Tech!" Then she paused and whispered, "As for Dr. Troy's lab—enter at your own risk!" The security officer gave a short laugh.

Just then they heard footsteps at the office door.

Chapter · 2

"Well, it's about time you got here," a voice said gruffly. Tanya rose from her seat and turned towards the door of the security office. Ms. Fletcher looked away and busied herself at her desk.

Dr. Troy stood in the doorway, tall and straight, with her hair in a tight bun. Her hands were on her hips and her expression was definitely not friendly.

Tanya felt the blood rush to her face. She hated to start off on the wrong foot.

"Well, let's not waste any more time," Dr. Troy snapped. "Come on, I'll show you around." She turned on her heels and strode down the hall. Tanya

followed behind at a quick pace, trying to keep up.

Tanya searched for landmarks, so she could get her bearings. But all the hallways seemed identical. The walls were painted a dull gray. The floors were covered in a slightly darker industrial carpet.

"In this hall is the elevator that takes you up to the cafeteria," explained Dr. Troy. "The room with the copier and fax machine is down there at the end. I guess it's old-fashioned, but I like to have paper copies of my research. I'm probably the only one here who uses the copier. Besides, you never know who could be snooping around in your computer files," Dr. Troy said with a frown.

Dr. Troy continued with the quick tour. "The women's room is around that corner to your left."

Tanya's mind raced as she tried hard to follow Dr. Troy's rapid speech and pointing fingers. She concentrated on remembering where everything was.

Finally they came to a metal door. The nameplate on the door read: DR. KATHERINE TROY. AUTHORIZED PERSONNEL ONLY.

"You and I are the only ones who

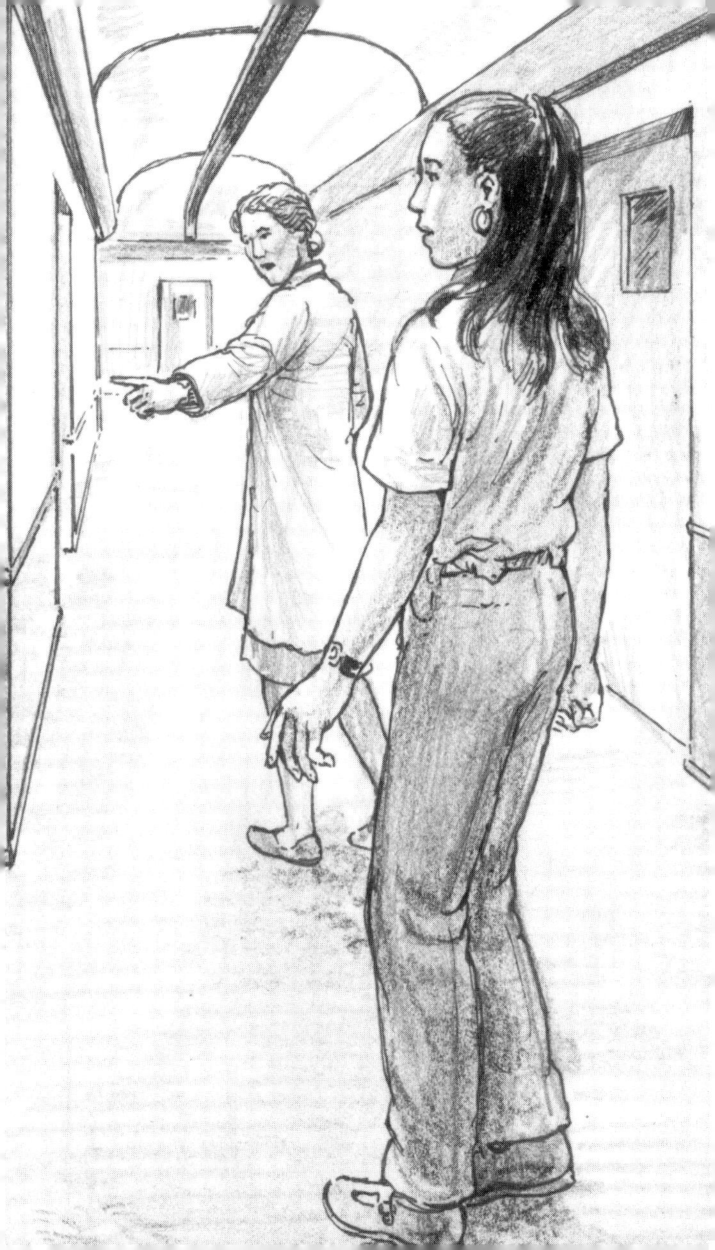

have access to my laboratory," Dr. Troy said. She pressed her badge against the security plate next to the door.

The door clicked open. Dr. Troy held the door with one hand and turned to face Tanya. She looked very serious. "I expect you to live up to the trust that I have placed in you. You are my personal assistant. That means that you report to me and only to me. Is that understood?"

"Yes, Dr. Troy," Tanya answered

nervously. Her new boss was tough!

"Good." Dr. Troy pushed the heavy door open and walked in. She hit a switch on the wall and the room was flooded with light.

The laboratory was as large as Tanya's classroom back at school. There were two desks, each with a computer. There was a sink in a far corner of the room.

The rest of the room was filled with cases and cases of bugs.

Chapter · 3

Tanya knew that Dr. Troy was an entomologist, a scientist who studies insects. But she didn't expect there to be so many bugs to study!

The glass cases magnified the size of the bugs. Tanya could clearly see their large eyes and waving antennae.

Dr. Troy handed Tanya a notebook. "I need you to make copies of the last three pages in this book."

Tanya took the notebook and left the lab.

"Copier," she muttered to herself, as if saying the word would make the copier magically appear.

She remembered the copier was in a room at the end of one hall, but which one? Tanya stopped and tried one of the unlocked doors. She had her hand on the doorknob when suddenly the door swung open. James stepped out.

"Hi," he said. James seemed surprised to see the intern.

"I'm, uh, looking for the copier," Tanya stammered.

"Well, it wasn't in here last time I checked," he said.

Tanya looked at the door and realized that she had almost walked into the men's room by mistake. She blushed.

"Come on," smiled James. "I'll show

you where the copier is. Follow me."

James led Tanya around the corner into a small, windowless room.

"So, how's your first day going?" James asked. He turned on the copier and it started to hum.

"Not so good," Tanya replied honestly. "Dr. Troy was upset that I was late, even though I actually got here early." It was a relief to talk to someone about her feelings.

Tanya opened the notebook to the last few pages and pressed the book down on the glass top of the copier.

"I wouldn't take it personally," said James. "Dr. Troy has a quick temper. If she weren't so smart, I don't think Gen-Tech would put up with her tantrums." Tanya smiled at James's comforting words.

As she flipped to the next page, a sheet of paper slipped out of the notebook and fell to the floor.

"I've got it," said James. He picked it up and handed it to Tanya.

"Thanks." Tanya scanned the page, wondering if it was one that she was supposed to copy. It was a letter from the Entomological Society of Canada. The letter read:

Dear Dr. Troy,

> *Since you were not able to provide the specimens you had expected to submit, we have no choice but to reject your grant application.*

Regretfully,

Dr. Lloyd Thompson

Executive Director

Tanya was flustered. She didn't know if she should copy the letter or not. She decided to make a copy just to be on the safe side.

"All done?" asked James as Tanya gathered the copies from the paper tray.

"Yes, thanks," she said. "I'd better hurry back. Dr. Troy's waiting for these."

"See you later," James said as they left the copy room.

"I hope so," Tanya found herself thinking as she walked back to Dr. Troy's lab.

Tanya fumbled for her ID badge, then she let herself into the lab.

"What took you so long?" asked Dr. Troy. She glared at Tanya.

"I got lost," explained Tanya. "But James helped me find the right room."

27

"In the future, do your flirting on your own time," Dr. Troy said sharply.

Tanya was determined not to let her new boss get to her. But it wasn't easy. "Here are the copies you wanted," she replied evenly.

Dr. Troy flipped through the copies. She stopped when she reached the copy

of the letter from the Entomological Society.

"Why did you copy this?" the scientist asked angrily. She ripped the piece of paper to bits. It tumbled from her hands like confetti.

"It . . . f—fell out of your notebook," Tanya stuttered.

"I don't know why I saved that letter," Dr. Troy said in a softer voice. Her anger of a moment before was replaced by sadness. "I guess I kept it to remind me of my new goal."

"Your new goal?" repeated Tanya. "You mean your research work here at Gen-Tech?"

Dr. Troy laughed. "My work for Gen-Tech is just a small part of my work. You see all these insects?" Dr. Troy gestured toward the cases of bugs. "These are nothing compared to my real work . . . my secret project that will finally bring me my revenge!"

Chapter · 4

Secret work? Revenge? Tanya was curious. But she had seen enough of Dr. Troy's temper to know that she shouldn't press her for more details.

For the rest of the day, Tanya settled into the tasks that would become her daily job. Her work in the lab consisted of keeping the cases clean and monitoring the insects. Then Tanya entered her observations about the insects on the computer.

There were many different species. Tanya was stunned by how all these different animals could be lumped together into one category: *insects*.

But Dr. Troy reminded Tanya of one of the first things the girl had learned in biology—all insects have some important things in common.

"Every insect has six legs. And an insect's body is divided into three parts," Dr. Troy said. "The first section is its head, which contains a tiny brain, eyes, long thin feelers called antennae, and the insect's mouth."

Dr. Troy pulled a magnifying lens out from a drawer and invited Tanya to examine one of the insects.

She continued with her speech. "The middle section is called the thorax. That includes three pairs of legs and usually two pairs of wings. Finally, there's the rear section, which consists of the abdomen. The abdomen carries the organs for digesting food, breathing, mating, and, in females, laying eggs."

Tanya listened quietly as she studied the insect. She had read about insects in her biology textbook. But being in a real working lab was so much better!

"So, that's that," said Dr. Troy. "I'll leave you to your work. I have some other experiments I need to attend to." Dr. Troy took a pad and pencil from her desk and went to the back of the lab. With a key, she opened a door marked "SUPPLIES" and went inside. The door closed behind her. Tanya thought she

heard the lock click as if Dr. Troy had locked herself inside.

Tanya finished a complete round of the insect cases and sat down at her desk to record the data on her computer. By the time she was finished,

Tanya was startled to see that it was almost three o'clock.

Tanya took out her lunch from her brand new briefcase. Her grandmother had surprised her with the briefcase as a gift that morning.

Just as Tanya finished eating, the

phone rang at her desk. "Hello," Tanya said, "Dr. Troy's lab."

"Is Dr. Troy there?"

"She's busy in another lab right now," Tanya answered. "May I take a message?"

"I'm glad the good doctor is nice and busy." The voice sounded familiar to Tanya. "That means you can talk."

"James?" Tanya was pleased that James was thinking of her. But then she remembered what Dr. Troy had said about flirting.

"I just wanted to see if your first day was getting any better."

"It's going okay, I guess," said Tanya.

"Dr. Troy isn't making your life too miserable?"

"Well, she did chain me to my desk," Tanya joked, "but she said she would unlock me at five o'clock."

"Good," James said. "I could give you a ride home today, if you'd like."

Tanya hesitated. She hardly knew James. There was a moment of awkward silence.

"I, uh, saw your address on the forms you filled out," James explained, "and it's on my way to school. I take night classes at the community college. I have to be there at six."

"Well, sure," said Tanya. "Thanks. That would be great."

"Okay! Just stop by my desk when you're ready."

After Tanya hung up the phone, she felt refreshed.

The rest of the day flew by. At five o'clock, Dr. Troy emerged from the back of her lab. She looked tired. The neat bun she'd worn that morning had begun to come undone. Several loose strands of hair hung down the side of her face.

Tanya felt a wave of sympathy for Dr. Troy. She obviously worked very hard. Maybe she wasn't the friendliest person in the world. But, so what?

"Quitting time," Dr. Troy said as she dropped her notepad on her desk. She sank wearily into her chair and started pounding away on her computer keyboard.

Dr. Troy didn't look up from her work. "See you tomorrow, Tanya. Don't be late."

Chapter · 5

Tanya's first couple of weeks at Gen-Tech went pretty much like her first day.

She worked hard and learned more and more about insects. Every day at five o'clock, Tanya went upstairs where James was waiting to drive her home on his way to school. Often she was loaded down with books Dr. Troy loaned her to read in the evenings.

In the morning, no matter how early Tanya came to work, Dr. Troy was always there before her. Sometimes Dr. Troy's hair would be messy, as if she had worked all night and never gone home.

Dr. Troy was clearly pleased with

Tanya's interest and hard work. She started talking to Tanya each morning as she drank her coffee. It became their morning routine.

Usually their talks focused on what

needed to be done that day. But sometimes, Dr. Troy told Tanya stories about her field work.

Several months a year, Dr. Troy travelled to rain forests all over the world looking for rare species of insects to bring back and study.

She would set up a very simple campsite in a forest, and spend long hours every day searching for particular insects.

One morning, Dr. Troy told her about searching for insects in the South American rain forest.

"Don't the mosquitoes bother you?" asked Tanya.

A dark scowl crossed Dr. Troy's face. "Mosquitoes!" repeated Dr. Troy. Her voice was laced with hatred. "I detest mosquitoes."

"Me, too," said Tanya lightly. "I'm always getting bitten."

"Those awful mosquitoes cost me a

million dollar grant." Dr. Troy's eyes blazed with fury.

Tanya remembered the letter from the Entomological Society of Canada that had fallen out of Dr. Troy's notebook. "What happened?" she asked.

"On one of my trips I had just found an extremely rare insect specimen," Dr. Troy said in a strained voice. "One that was thought to have been extinct. I spotted it on a leaf and was just about to capture it when a huge swarm of mosquitoes came buzzing around my head. They were biting my face and scalp. I couldn't see, they were so thick around me!"

Dr. Troy started to wave her hands in front of her face as if she were reliving the experience right there in the lab.

"By the time I regained control, the

insect I wanted was gone," the scientist said angrily.

"Couldn't you find another one?" asked Tanya.

"Collecting certain insects is like finding a needle in a haystack," explained Dr. Troy. "I searched for weeks. Finally, my supplies ran out and I had to return. I told the Entomological Society about my find, but because I didn't have proof, they denied my grant. All because of those mosquitoes." Dr. Troy's face flushed red with anger. "I hate mosquitoes!"

Tanya felt sorry for Dr. Troy. She had worked so hard and all for nothing. No wonder she hated mosquitoes.

"That reminds me," said Dr. Troy. She seemed back in control of her emotions. "I was wondering if you'd like to help me with a special project."

"Sure!" said Tanya immediately. She was eager to do more than just monitor the insects and clean up the lab.

"It's confidential. No one at Gen-Tech knows about it, and I want to keep it that way. You must promise not to tell anyone else about it."

"All right," Tanya agreed. But it seemed strange to her that Dr. Troy would keep her work secret even from her peers at Gen-Tech.

Dr. Troy led Tanya to the back of the lab. She unlocked the door marked "SUPPLIES" and flipped on the light switch.

At first, the small room seemed to be an extension of the rest of the lab. Cases of insects lined the walls. But on closer examination, Tanya realized that all the cases were filled with mosquitoes in different stages of development.

There were cases of adult mosquitoes. There were also cases filled with water and mosquito eggs, called larvae. Some of the larvae floated in clumps on the surface. Others wriggled to the bottom of the water as Tanya's shadow passed over the case.

On the walls were large blown-up photographs of mosquitoes. The photos showed every detail of the adult mosquito: its sucking mouth sticking out of the front of its face; the two

bristly antennae pointing out toward the sides. The big eyes behind the antennae looked like two bunches of small bumps. Magnified like this, the mosquito looked like a fearsome monster. It was horrible and fascinating at the same time.

"Are you breeding mosquitoes?" the young intern asked.

Dr. Troy shuddered. "These mosquitoes are simply tools for helping me reach my goal." Dr. Troy led Tanya to a separate case in a corner of the small lab. "This is my creation . . . my Megabug!"

Tanya looked into the case and saw a brightly colored beetlelike bug about the size of a penny. When the light hit the bug, its back reflected all the colors of the rainbow. "It's beautiful!" whispered Tanya in awe.

"The Megabug's coloring acts as a natural defense," explained Dr. Troy

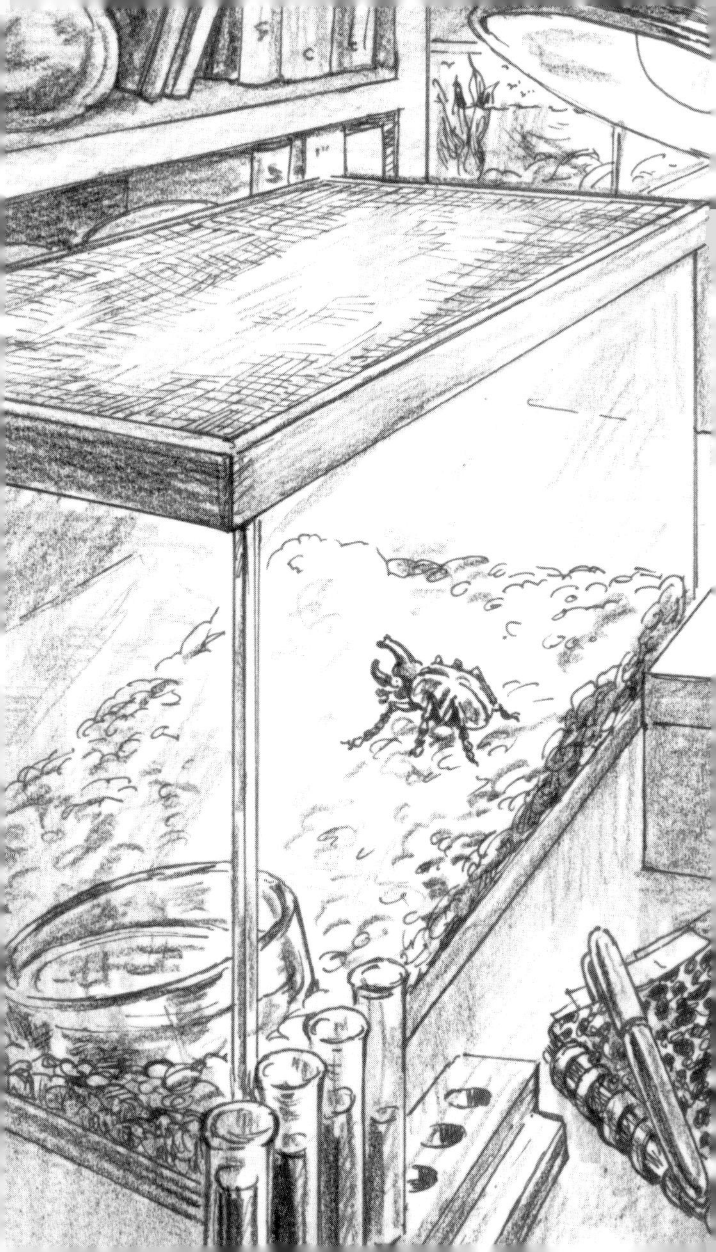

proudly. "Brightly colored insects tend to be poisonous, so other animals know to stay away from them."

Tanya marveled at the Megabug. "You created a new species of insect? That's amazing! But why keep it a secret?"

"Because I didn't create the Megabug to study it, or to get a grant from the Entomological Society." Dr. Troy spat out the words as if they left a bad taste in her mouth. "I created the Megabug with one purpose in mind: to eat mosquitoes . . . all the mosquitoes! When I release it, the Megabug will rid this planet of mosquitoes forever!"

Chapter · 6

Dr. Troy's eyes widened with excitement as she spoke of her Megabug. It was as if her whole personality had changed when she stepped into this secret lab. To Tanya it was like watching Dr. Jekyll and Mr. Hyde, and it really frightened her.

But Tanya was also flattered that Dr. Troy trusted her enough to share this secret experiment. She wanted to show Dr. Troy she was worthy of that trust. Still, something about Dr. Troy's experiment with the Megabug bothered her. Tanya tried to push those thoughts from her mind.

Dr. Troy explained what she wanted Tanya to do. In addition to her work in the regular lab, Dr. Troy asked Tanya to supervise the breeding of the mosquitoes so that the Megabug would have plenty of food.

Dr. Troy explained that she had been feeding the Megabug mosquito larvae. Now it was eating adult mosquitoes as well.

The Megabug could walk on water and suck up the larvae through its long beaklike mouth. It could also trap adult mosquitoes in its pincer-like front legs.

But what was truly amazing about Dr. Troy's Megabug was its appetite. The Megabug was always hungry. It was eating almost a pound of mosquito larvae a day—and the bug was growing larger. That's why Dr. Troy had named it the Megabug, because *mega* means large.

Dr. Troy wanted Tanya to care for and monitor the Megabug. That way Dr. Troy would be able to devote her time to creating a second Megabug. Then, the two Megabugs could mate and produce mosquito-eating offspring.

Tanya quickly settled into the new

routine. But taking care of both labs kept her very busy. Tanya often worked straight through lunch. It was the only way that she could finish by five o'clock and drive home with James.

Lately, James did most of the talking as they drove. He told Tanya about his classes. He was studying meteorology, so he could report the weather on TV.

James had graduated from high school the previous year. He lived at

home and saved most of his salary. If his grades were good enough, he planned to transfer to a four-year college next year.

Tanya understood the pressure to make money to pay for school. In her interview with Dr. Troy, Tanya had explained that she could only accept this unpaid internship at Gen-Tech if it would help her qualify for a full college scholarship. Otherwise, like James, she would have to work at odd jobs to pay her tuition.

Dr. Troy had promised Tanya that she would help her get a full scholarship to whatever university she wanted to attend. The scientist had assured Tanya that she was on the Boards of Directors of many colleges. A letter of recommendation from Dr. Troy would really help Tanya out.

Several weeks after Tanya started working at Gen-Tech, James asked her out on a real date. Tanya was thrilled. She rushed through her front door that evening to tell her grandmother the news. She hoped it would lift her grandmother's spirits.

Tanya knew her grandmother had been worried about her lately. Tanya had lost her appetite when she started working on Dr. Troy's secret project. She just couldn't manage to eat lunch after watching the Megabug gobble up mosquitoes all morning.

Besides losing weight, Tanya hadn't been sleeping well either. She had nightmares about mosquitoes. And she had a recurring dream about the Megabug, too. In the dream, the Megabug had grown as big as a horse. Dr. Troy was riding the bug like a cowboy, chasing after her. Tanya knew that if it caught her, it would gobble her up like a mosquito larva.

After several of Tanya's sleepless

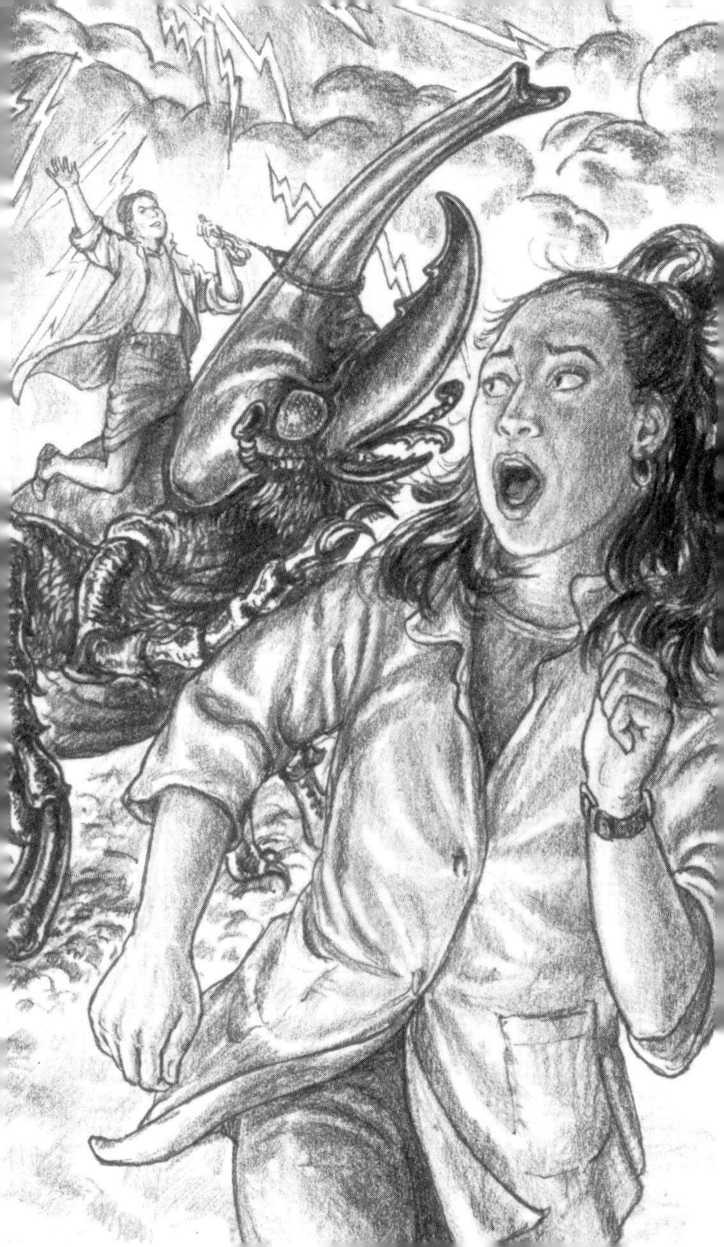

nights, her grandmother commented about the dark circles under her granddaughter's eyes.

Tanya wanted to confide in her grandmother, but she had promised Dr. Troy not to mention the secret project to anyone.

If Dr. Troy found out the teen had betrayed her, Tanya could kiss her scholarship goodbye. All her hard work would have been for nothing. Her dreams of college and a degree in biology would be in danger!

But the night of the date, Tanya's energy was up. Her grandmother helped Tanya pick out a perfect outfit. She loaned her a special shawl that Tanya wrapped around her shoulders. It made Tanya look even lovelier than she already was.

"You look beautiful," said her grandmother. "Just like your mother when she was your age."

Tanya couldn't remember the last time her grandmother had mentioned her mother. Tanya sensed her grandmother must have something important on her mind.

"What is it, Grandma?" asked Tanya. She figured her grandmother wanted to talk to her about boys. Even though they'd had this discussion several times before, Tanya prepared herself to listen to it again. She waited patiently.

But her grandmother had other concerns about Tanya.

"Are you dieting?" she asked.

"No, Grandma," answered Tanya. "I've just been so busy at work, I haven't had time to eat lunch."

"It's not healthy for a young woman to be so thin," she said. "I will make you special lunches every day and you must promise me that you will eat them."

"Okay, Grandma," said Tanya, "I promise."

"Good." Her grandmother smiled warmly. "Now, let's do your hair."

When James picked Tanya up for their date, he was struck speechless by how beautiful she looked. He stood frozen at the door and stared for a moment before Tanya led him inside to meet her grandmother.

After a movie, James took Tanya to a coffee shop. For awhile they talked about the movie. Then the conversation turned to Gen-Tech.

"So, rumor has it that Dr. Troy is working on some extra-secret project," said James casually.

Tanya almost choked on her veggieburger. "What do you mean?" she asked.

"People at work were talking about some unusual shipments she received,"

James said, "and that she's spending nights working in her lab. So what's going on?"

Tanya's promise to Dr. Troy ran through her mind. She hated to lie, especially to James. So she tried to avoid his question instead. "She does work very hard . . . which reminds me," said Tanya, trying to change the subject. "How is your work going?"

Fortunately, James seemed just as happy to talk about his own work as Dr. Troy's. Tanya was relieved that he didn't press her to tell him what was really going on in the lab. She was afraid that with more encouragement she might have given in and told him everything.

The Monday after her date with James, Tanya was feeding the Megabug in the secret lab. With a start, she realized that the afternoon had come and she hadn't eaten her own lunch yet. She unwrapped the roast beef sandwich her grandmother had made for her and took a big bite. Some of the meat fell from her sandwich into the Megabug's case.

Before Tanya could retrieve it, the Megabug had gobbled it up. Tanya was horrified. It scared her to see how hungrily the Megabug tore at the meat. She worried about what might happen to the bug when it tried to digest it! And what would Dr. Troy do when she found

out what happened?

Tanya watched the Megabug for the rest of the afternoon. She was worried that it might die. Dr. Troy would surely fire her, and no university would want such a careless student in its science department.

Tanya couldn't sleep at all that night. What would she do if the bug was dead when she got to work tomorrow?

The next morning, her grandmother packed Tanya's lunch into her briefcase.

"What's in the sandwiches you make for me?" Tanya asked.

"I put a special dressing on the meat in your sandwich to increase your appetite and make you grow strong."

Tanya wondered how that might affect the Megabug.

When Tanya got to the lab, Dr. Troy was already there. She was standing over the Megabug case. "What have you been doing to this bug?" Dr. Troy asked.

"Oh, no," Tanya thought to herself. "She knows. I shouldn't have been eating in the secret lab!"

Before Tanya could confess, Dr. Troy hugged her. "Well, whatever it is, you're doing a great job. The Megabug is really growing! It's amazing!"

But Tanya wasn't so happy. If the Megabug ate roast beef, it might eat all kinds of meat. That afternoon she decided to conduct her own experiment.

Tanya fed the Megabug a piece of chicken from her sandwich. The Megabug devoured it greedily.

The next day, Tanya gave it a piece of ham with the same results.

Just as she feared, the Megabug thrived on all kinds of meat. And it was growing! Just that week, the bug had swelled until it was almost the size of Tanya's palm.

Tanya calculated that at its current rate of growth, the Megabug would be the size of a cat in less than a month. And it would have the appetite of a lion with a taste for meat.

Any meat.

Perhaps even the meat of human beings!

Chapter · 7

The more the Megabug grew, the more impatient Dr. Troy became to release it.

Dr. Troy gleefully watched the Megabug devour mosquitoes. She actually cheered as if she were at a ballgame rooting for her home team.

Tanya was really alarmed now. She voiced her concerns about the harm this new species could cause to the environment. But Dr. Troy refused to listen to criticism of her master plan.

Dr. Troy had almost completed her work to create a second Megabug. Soon the two Megabugs would mate and their offspring would munch on all the mosquitoes in the world!

Tanya was convinced that it would be a disaster if the Megabugs were released. But what could she do? No one would take the word of a summer intern against that of a well-known scientist.

And if she "accidentally" killed the Megabug, Dr. Troy would almost surely fire her. Tanya would lose her scholarship and Dr. Troy would simply create another Megabug.

But Tanya couldn't just stand by and do nothing. The stakes were too high.

That night, she told her grandmother everything. When she was done, there was a moment of thoughtful silence.

Finally, Tanya's grandmother spoke. "I think the Megabug reacted to the growth medicine I put in your sandwich. Although I have never tried to use medicine on bugs, tomorrow I

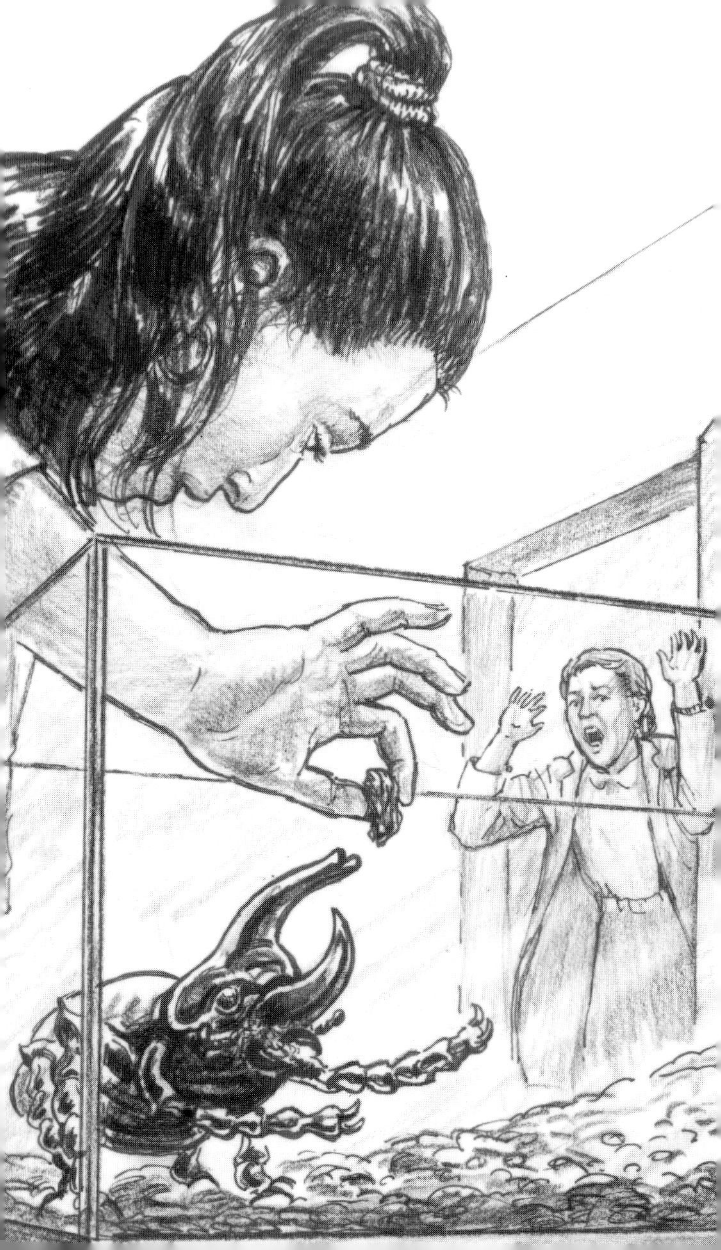

will make one that causes a loss of appetite. We can only hope it will work its natural way on that unnatural bug."

The next day, Tanya brought a special "lunch" for the Megabug. She waited for Dr. Troy to leave the secret lab. Then she dropped it inside the case.

"What are you doing?" Dr. Troy shouted as she returned to the lab unexpectedly. She reached inside the case to take out the food.

"Wait!" Tanya warned as the Megabug quickly crawled to the piece of meat. But Dr. Troy had already grabbed hold of the meat. The Megabug scrambled after its snack, and crawled right onto the scientist's hand.

The bug quickly gobbled the meat Dr. Troy held between her fingers—but it didn't stop there.

"Yeow!" screamed Dr. Troy.

The Megabug had taken a giant bite out of her hand.

Chapter · 8

Dr. Troy spun around in pain. She knocked one of the lab cases to the floor where it landed with a crash. The glass shattered and hundreds of adult mosquitoes swarmed around her.

"Help!" Dr. Troy screamed. She waved her arms furiously at the buzzing insects. In her confusion, she knocked another case to the ground. More mosquitoes were released.

Blinded by the buzzing swarm, Dr. Troy backed into a table. It collapsed, sending all her special equipment crashing to the floor.

Tanya watched in horror as the

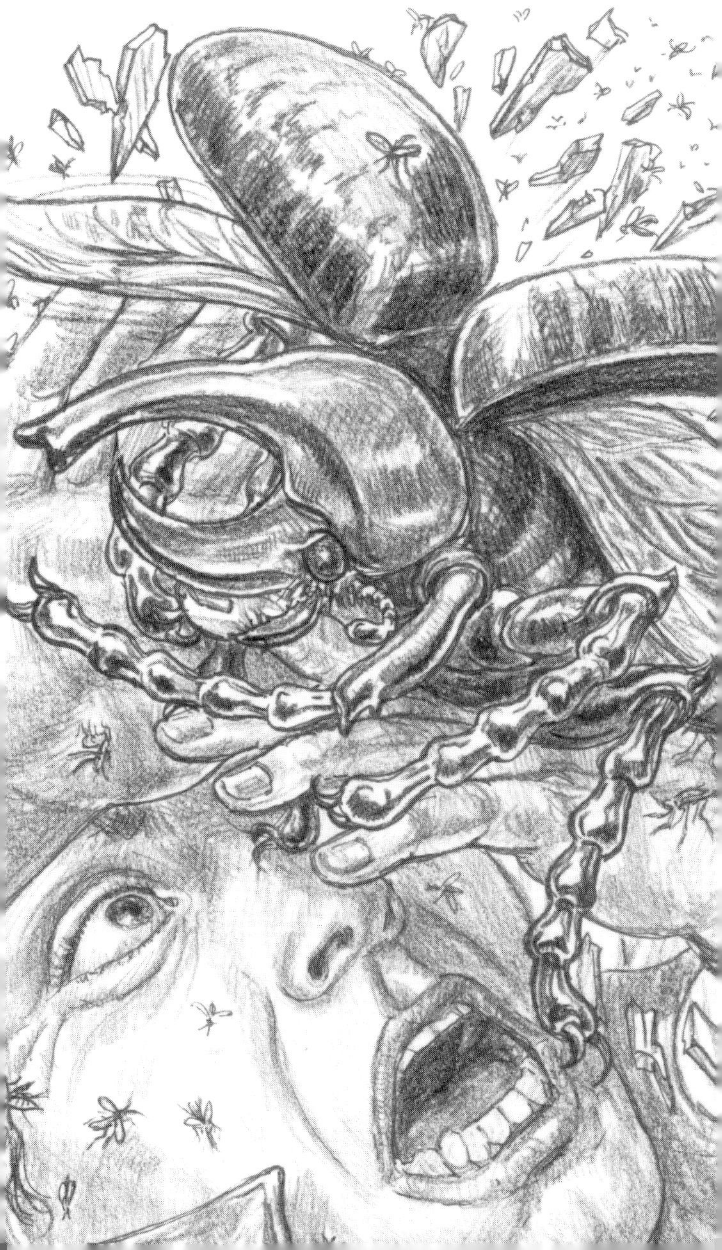

mosquitoes swarmed around her and Dr. Troy. The Megabug was now feasting on the mosquitoes that landed on the scientist's hand. And it kept chewing Dr. Troy's fingers!

"Tanya! Do something!" screamed Dr. Troy.

Tanya grabbed Dr. Troy's notebook off the desk and quickly swept the Megabug off of Dr. Troy's hand. Then, knowing she had no choice, Tanya squashed the Megabug with her foot.

Dr. Troy screamed. "You've killed it! You stupid girl! You killed my bug!" She collapsed onto the floor, sobbing uncontrollably.

Dr. Troy slumped against a wall. She picked up what remained of the Megabug. Its yellow blood oozed out onto her hand. "Oh, my bug!" she cried.

Tanya looked around her. The lab was in ruins. Mosquitoes were swarming everywhere. She spotted a fire alarm

and pulled down the lever. Immediately the room was showered with water from the sprinklers in the ceiling. She heard the dull wail of a siren and waited for help to come.

***

***

The late summer sun streamed through the open window of James's car and warmed Tanya's arms.

Tanya couldn't believe she was actually on her way to one of Canada's top universities on a full scholarship. After what happened at Dr. Troy's lab, she had been sure her scientific career was over before it could begin.

But the head of Gen-Tech had written

to the university himself. He secured a scholarship for Tanya based on her attempts to prevent Dr. Troy's experiment from succeeding. The director was concerned that Tanya hadn't reported the problem right away. But he had understood the intern's dilemma. He praised Tanya for her concerns about what might happen if the Megabug were released, and for her attempts to solve the problem. Tanya

had acted as a good scientist should.

And now James, her boyfriend, was driving her to school to begin her freshman year of college.

"Are you sure you want to stop to see Dr. Troy on your way?" asked James.

"Yes," said Tanya with more certainty than she felt. "It's the next exit."

Dr. Troy had suffered a nervous breakdown. She spent most of Tanya's senior year of high school in the hospital. Tanya had written her several letters, but had received no replies.

Tanya found out that Dr. Troy had been moved to a place that was near the university where Tanya was enrolled. The girl decided to visit.

James pulled into the parking lot of the rest home. "I'll wait for you in the car," he said.

Tanya gave him a quick kiss. She grabbed a big box of chocolates she had brought as a gift and went inside.

When she knocked on the door to Dr. Troy's room, a frail voice called out, "Come in."

Tanya entered. "I must be in the wrong room," she thought to herself as her eyes rested on the woman lying quietly in the bed.

Dr. Troy did not look healthy. Her long gray hair hung limply along the sides of her thin face.

"Please close the door," said the woman. "I don't want any bugs to get in."

Tanya quickly closed the door behind her. "Hello, Dr. Troy. It's me, Tanya Redfeather. How are you feeling?"

"Oh, I'd be just fine if it weren't for these mosquitoes." Dr. Troy waved her hands in front of her head, trying to swat invisible mosquitoes. "As soon as the buzzing stops I'll be able to get back to my work." Dr. Troy pulled the covers over her head to block out the imaginary noise.

Tanya was stunned. There wasn't a single mosquito in the room. She waited a minute, but Dr. Troy seemed to have fallen asleep underneath her cover.

Tanya gently pulled the cover off the doctor's head. Then she left the box of

chocolates on the table.

In the hall, Tanya asked a nurse how Dr. Troy was doing. "Oh, she's actually much better," said the nurse. "We've seen cases like this before. Some people crack under all the pressure of their jobs. They can really suffer a lot from the stress. It'll take time."

Reassured by the nurse's words, Tanya walked back outside to James's car. "I'll just have to make sure I don't get that carried away with my own work!" she thought.

As she got into the car, a mosquito landed on her right arm. She crushed it with her left hand and flicked the dead bug away.

James started the car and Tanya headed off to start her new life at the university.